RUDOLPH

THE RED-NOSED REINDEER

Written for

MONTGOMERY WARD

by

ROBERT L. MAY

ILLUSTRATED BY DENVER GILLEN

FACSIMILE EDITION

APPLEWOOD BOOKS
Carlisle, Massachusetts

'TWAS the day before Christmas, and all through the hills

The reindeer were playing . . . enjoying the spills

Of skating and coasting, and climbing the willows . . .

And hop-scotch and leap-frog (<u>protected</u> by <u>pillows!</u>)

While every so often they'd stop to call names

At one little deer not allowed in their games:—

"Ha ha! Look at Rudolph! His nose is a sight!"

"It's red as a beet!" "Twice as <u>big!</u>" "Twice as <u>bright!</u>"

While Rudolph just wept.

What <u>else</u> could he do?

He <u>knew</u> that the things

they were saying were true!

WHERE most reindeers' noses are brownish and tiny,

Poor Rudolph's was red, very large, and quite shiny.

In daylight it dazzled. (The picture shows that!)

At night-time it glowed, like the eyes of a cat.

And putting dirt on it just made it look muddy.

(Oh boy was he mad when they nick-named him "Ruddy!")

Although he was lonesome, he always was good . . .

Obeying his parents, as <u>good</u> reindeer should!

That's <u>why</u>, on this day, Rudolph <u>almost</u> felt playful:—

He hoped that from <u>Santa</u> (soon driving his sleighful

Of presents and candy and dollies and toys

For <u>good</u> little animals, good girls and boys)

He'd get <u>just</u> as much . . . and <u>this</u> is what pleased him . . .

As the happier, handsomer reindeer who teased him.

So as night, and a fog,

   hid the world like a hood,

He went to bed hopeful;

   he <u>knew</u> he'd been good!

WHILE WAY, way up North, on this <u>same</u> foggy night,

Old Santa was packing his sleigh for its flight.

"This fog," he complained, "will be hard to get through!"

He shook his round head. (And his <u>tummy</u> shook, too!)

"Without any stars or a moon as our compass,

This extra-dark night is quite likely to swamp us.

To keep from collisions, we'll have to fly slow.

To keep our direction, we'll have to fly low.

We'll steer by street-lamps and houses tonight,

In order to finish before it gets light.

Just think how the boys' and girls'

    faith would be shaken,

If <u>we</u> <u>didn't</u> reach 'em

    before they awaken!

C OME DASHER! Come Dancer! Come Prancer and Vixen!

Come Comet! Come Cupid! Come Donner and Blitzen!

Be quick with your suppers! Get hitched in a hurry!

You, <u>too</u>, will find fog a delay and a worry!"

And Santa was right. (As he usually is!)

The fog was as thick as a soda's white fizz

Just NOT-getting-LOST needed all Santa's skill . . .

With street-signs and numbers more difficult still.

He tangled in tree-tops again and again,

And barely missed hitting a tri-motored plane.

He <u>still</u> made good speed, with much twisting and turning,

As long as the street lamps and house lights were burning.

At <u>each</u> house, first <u>noting</u> the people who live there,

He'd quickly select the right presents to give there.

By midnight, however, the last light had fled.

(For even <u>big</u> people have <u>then</u> gone to bed!)

BECAUSE it might wake them, a match was denied him.

(Oh <u>my</u>, how he wished for just <u>one</u> star to guide him!)

Through <u>dark</u> streets and houses old Santa fared poorly.

He <u>now</u> picked the presents more slowly, less surely.

He really was worried! For <u>what</u> would he do,

If folks started waking before he was through?

The air was still foggy,

the night dark and drear,

When Santa arrived

at the home of the deer.

A ledge that he tripped-on while seeking the chimney
Gave Santa a spill, and a painfully skinned-knee.

The room he came down in

was blacker than ink,

He went for a chair,

and then found it . . . a sink!

The first reindeer bedroom

was so very black,

He tripped on the rug,

and fell flat on his back.

So dark that he had to move close to the bed,

And squint very hard at the sleeping deer's head,

Before he could choose

the right kind of a toy.

(A doll for a girl,

or a train for a boy.)

B ut all this took time, and filled Santa with gloom,

While slowly he groped toward the next reindeer's room

The door he'd just opened . . . when, to his surprise,

A dim but quite definite light met his eyes.

The lamp wasn't burning; the glow came, instead,

From something that lay at the head of the bed.

And there lay . . . but wait now! What would you suppose?

The glowing (you've guessed it) was *RUDOLPH'S*

RED

NOSE.

So <u>this</u> room was easy!

This <u>one</u> little light

Let Santa pick quickly

the gifts that were right.

How <u>happy</u> he was, till he went out the door . . .

The <u>rest</u> of the house was as black as <u>before</u>!

So black that it made

every step a dark mystery.

And <u>then</u> . . . came the greatest

idea in all history!

He went back to Rudolph

and started to shake him

(Of course, very gently)

in order to wake him.

And Rudolph could scarcely believe his own eyes!

You just can imagine his joy and surprise

At seeing who stood there, so real and so near,

While telling the tale we've already told here:—

Poor Santa's sad tale of distress and delay . . .

The fog and the darkness, and losing the way . . .

The horrible fear that some children might waken

Before his complete Christmas trip had been taken.

"AND YOU," he told Rudolph, "may <u>yet</u> save the day!

Your wonderful forehead may <u>yet</u> pave the way

For a wonderful triumph! It actually might!"

(Old Santa, you notice, was extra-polite

To Rudolph, regarding his "wonderful forehead."

To call it a "big, shiny nose" would sound horrid!)

"I need you," said Santa, "to help me tonight . . .

To lead all my deer on the rest of our flight."

And Rudolph broke-out into <u>such</u> a big grin,

It almost connected his ears and his chin!

A note for his folks he dashed-off in a hurry.

"I've gone to help Santa, " he wrote. "Do not worry."

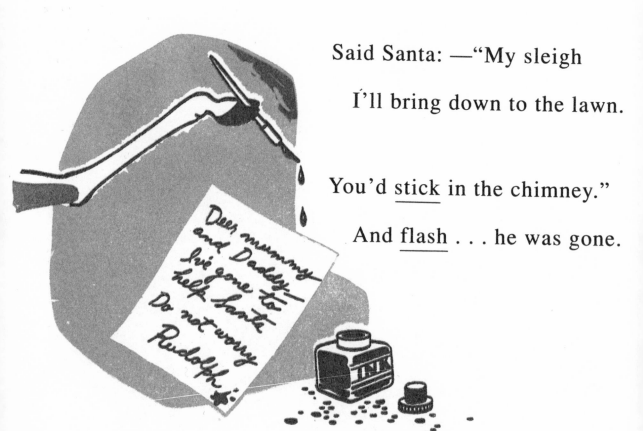

Said Santa: —"My sleigh

I'll bring down to the lawn.

You'd <u>stick</u> in the chimney."

And <u>flash</u> . . . he was gone.

S O RUDOLPH pranced-out through the door, very gay,

And took his proud place at the head of the sleigh.

The rest of the night . . . well, what would you guess?

Old Santa's idea was a brilliant success.

And "brilliant" was almost no word for the way

That Rudolph directed the deer and the sleigh.

IN spite of the fog, they flew quickly, and low,

And made such good use of the wonderful glow

From Rudolph's . . . er . . . forehead, at each intersection

That not even <u>once</u> did they lose their direction!

While <u>as</u> for the houses and streets with a sign on 'em,

They merely flew close, so that Rudolph could <u>shine</u> on 'em

To <u>tell</u> who lived where, and just what to give whom.

They'd fly by each window and peek in the room.

OLD Santa knew always which children were good,

And minded their parents, and ate as they should

So Santa selected the gift that was right,

While Rudolph's . . . er . . . forehead gave <u>just</u> enough light.

It all went so fast, that before it was day,

The very last present was given away . . .

The very last stocking was filled to the top,

<u>Just</u> as the sun was preparing to pop.

This sun woke the reindeer in Rudolph's home town.

They found the short message that he'd written down . . .

Then gathered outside to await his return.

And <u>were</u> they excited, astonished, to learn

That Rudolph, the ugliest deer of them all,

(Rudolph the Red-nose . . . bashful and small . . .

The funny-faced fellow they always called names,

And practically never allowed in their games)

Was now to be envied by all, far and near.

For no greater honor can come to a deer

Than riding with Santa and guiding his sleigh!

The number-one job, on the number-one day!

THE sleigh, and its reindeer, soon came into view.

And Rudolph still led them, as downward they flew.

Oh boy, was he proud, as they came to a landing

<u>Right</u> where his handsomer playmates were standing!

THESE bad deer who used to do nothing but tease him

Would now have done anything ... only to please him!

They felt even sorrier they had been bad

When Santa said:—"Rudolph, I never have had

A deer quite so brave or so brilliant as you

At fighting black fog, and at guiding me through.

By YOU last night's journey was actually bossed.

Without you, I'm certain we'd all have been lost!

I hope you'll continue to keep us from grief,

On future dark trips, as COMMANDER-IN-CHIEF!"

But Rudolph just blushed, from his head to his toes,

Until his <u>whole</u> fur was as red as his nose!

THE crowd first applauded, then started to screech:—

"Hurray for our Rudolph" and "We want a speech!"

But Rudolph was bashful, despite being a hero!

And tired! (His sleep on the trip totaled zero.)

So that's why his speech was just brief, and not bright:—

"Merry Christmas to all, and to all a good night" . . .

and THAT'S why . . . .

. . . . . . whenever it's foggy and gray,

It's Rudolph the Red-nose who guides Santa's sleigh.

Be listening, this Christmas! (But don't make a peep . . .

'cause <u>that</u> late at night, children <u>should</u> be asleep!)

The very first sound that you'll hear on the roof

(Provided there's fog) will be Rudolph's small hoof.

And soon after <u>that</u> (if you're still as a mouse)

You <u>may</u> hear a "swish" as he flies 'round the house,

And gives enough light to give Santa a view

Of you and your room. And <u>when</u> they're all through,

You _may_ hear them call, as they _drive_ out of sight:—

"MERRY CHRISTMAS TO ALL,
AND TO ALL
A GOOD NIGHT!"